Suddenly, on the rough path out of the village, in the darkness of the trees to our right, we heard a rustling. Grandfather stopped and listened. There was nothing.

"Maybe just a rabbit or something," he said. Still, he gripped my hand a little more tightly as we continued. As we approached our cottage, where Grandfather had left a lantern shining on the porch, there was another noise, and this time a voice spoke from behind us…

To Dad — R. K.
For Grandma — R. J.

Barefoot Books
2067 Massachusetts Ave
Cambridge, MA 02140

First published in the United States of America by Barefoot Books, Inc in 2009
This paperback edition first published in 2011

Graphic design by Graham Webb, Warminster, UK
Color Reproduction by B&P International, Hong Kong
Printed in China on 100% acid-free paper by Printplus, Ltd
This book was typeset in Carmina Light and Twilight
The illustrations were prepared in acrylics

ISBN 978-1-84686-624-1

Library of Congress Cataloging-in-Publication Data is
available under LCCN 2008028092

1 3 5 7 9 8 6 4 2

Winter Shadow

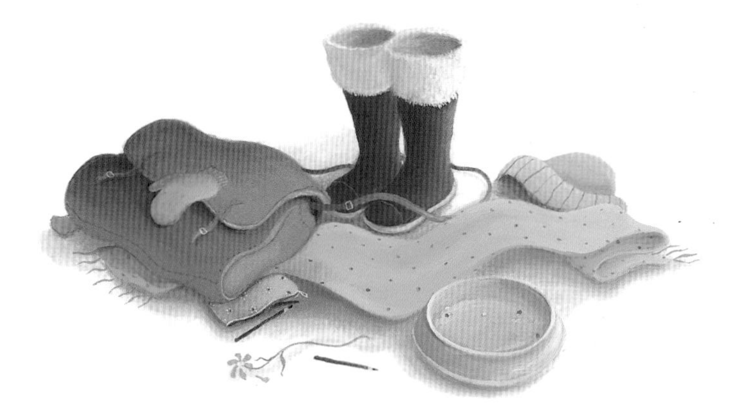

Written by
Richard Knight

Illustrated by
Richard Johnson

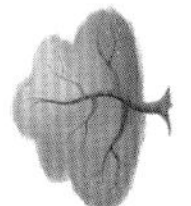

Contents

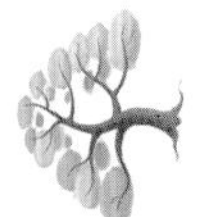

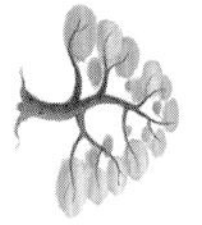

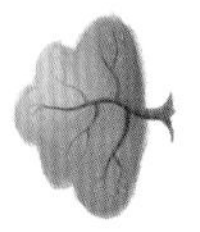
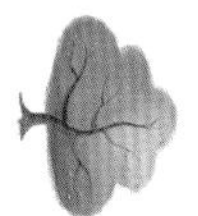

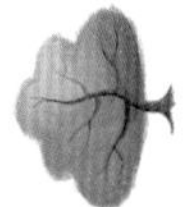 

 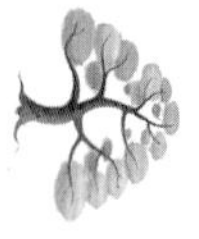

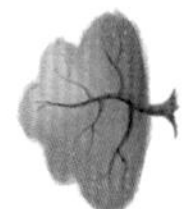 

Chapter One

The Discovery

SHADOW ARRIVED IN OUR LIVES unexpectedly on a cold winter's day and I loved him more than anything else, except perhaps for Grandfather himself. We lived in a small mountain village far away from the world beyond the flood plain, and we liked it that way. The winters were harsh, when the snow would cut us off from other villages for several months. But spring, when the snow melted and filled the streams and rivers of our valley, was always for us a time of celebration.

That morning I had kicked my way

through snow
as high as my
knees on the way
to school. The snows
had begun to fall every
night and I knew that
soon our lessons would
finish until the following
spring, and we children
would be free to spend
our days on our sleds on
the small slopes next to
the village school.

Everyone knew
about the wolves

in the forest but nobody was afraid of them. Years of experience told the villagers that respect and distance allowed us to live our lives, and the wolves theirs. So we did not fear them as other people might. We had even seen wolf pups before and watched them play, always from a safe distance, until they were called away by their mothers. At night, we could hear the plaintive calls of wolves among the mountains behind the village, but to us it was part of the music of the valley.

Yet that day as I kicked through the fresh, powdery snow I still felt a little dart of fear when I noticed a small gray bundle lying under a tree, half-covered in snow.

Chapter Two

Maria's Decision

The wisdom of the villagers told me to walk clear of it. A baby wolf is never far from its mother, and should she return, the mother would not wait to hear my excuses. I watched carefully. The wolf pup did not move. The forest whispered soft drops of snow to the ground. I was close enough to see one fall and

cling to the gray fur. Walking slowly backward, I continued on to school but kept watching to see if the pup would move. Then I lost sight of it as I rounded a bend in the path. Suddenly, I realized I would be late and ran the rest of the way, arriving just as the teacher was closing the door.

"Maria! Be quick, girl!"

The day dragged, more so than any other. Those last, long afternoons before the winter break, with the classroom almost in darkness, were hard enough for me. But on that afternoon I watched the large clock above the teacher's desk more closely than ever, urging its reluctant hands around. When the bell sounded at the end of the day, we children usually tumbled outside to play games in the snow before it became truly dark. But on that day after school, when I had told nobody about the wolf pup, I raced out of the door and across the schoolyard alone. The games in the snow were suddenly far from my mind as I hurried back along the same forest path. Perhaps the mother wolf had returned to find her pup and had carried it off to safety? Yet if the pup was still there, it may not have survived the bitterness of the day. I began to run faster, my heart racing.

Then, as I rounded the last bend, I saw him, perfectly still, snow now deep about his body. I swallowed hard and looked around, listening to the sounds of the forest, wondering what Grandfather would do. He was always certain of what was right; I knew that he would tell me to leave the pup there.

"That is nature, Maria. Leave him. You can do nothing for him."

My grandfather, who has always looked after me, spoke plainly and truthfully.

But that afternoon, with the light quickly fading above the silent forest, I blocked out his voice and picked the pup up in my arms. His eyes were closed and I suddenly panicked, thinking he might already be dead. He felt so cold. There was no sign of breathing, no beating of a warm heart.

Chapter Three

Will He Live?

I HURRIED HOME TO OUR COTTAGE and edged open the door to the kitchen, where the warmth and light and the smell of meat cooking welcomed me out of the winter darkness.

Grandfather turned from the stove and peered at me.

"What have you there, Maria?" He turned back to the pot he was stirring. "Is it from school?"

There was a long silence as I stood in the doorway, wondering how to answer.

I noticed his glasses lying on the kitchen table. For a moment, I thought about pretending to take an armful of wood to the shed, but Grandfather had taught me to be honest and I could not lie to him.

"It is a wolf pup. I found him in the woods. I think he is dying."

To my surprise, Grandfather didn't look at me straight away. Neither did he scold me. He replaced the heavy black lid on the pot and put the ladle on the table. Then he picked up his glasses and put them on.

"Well my girl. You set out the plates and let your grandfather see what can be done." He stretched out his strong arms, and I let the pup roll gently into them. Grandfather put him carefully on the table and studied the pup slowly, parting his fur, touching his skin in different places. Then he lowered his face and gently blew air into the pup's nose.

That evening we spent our time warming the pup slowly by the stove. He did not move, and we both sensed the fear that lay behind our silence. Grandfather said nothing about what I'd done until it was time for bed.

"You go now, Maria. If you have acted wisely and he lives, then tomorrow we will set him back where his mother may find him. And let us hope that it is *tomorrow* that she finds him." He stood and looked out of the window at the snow falling heavily among the trees before pulling the curtains across. I did not understand what he meant.

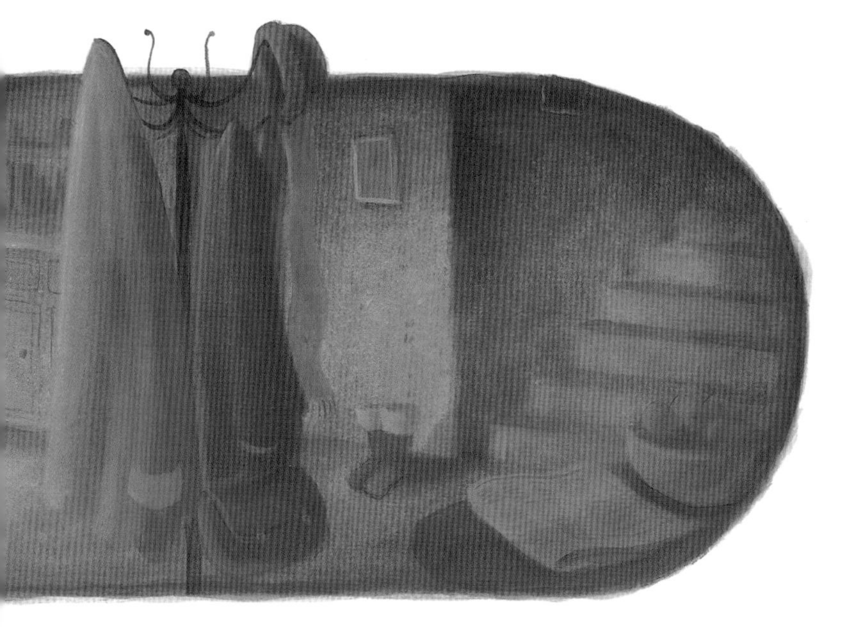

CHAPTER FOUR

THE ARGUMENT

THE MORNING CAME with fresh snow on the hillsides, and I went down to the warm kitchen.

"Maria, I have news." Grandfather, who was still sitting by the stove and looking tired, opened his corduroy jacket, and I could see a small, black nose inside. "He is alive." We smiled at each other.

That day at school I could not concentrate. I waited only for the bell that meant I could go home and see Shadow, for that is what I had decided to call the pup. Yet when I returned home, Grandfather's face was solemn.

"I took him back to the woods today. He is better off with his mother. He will survive; you have made sure of that."

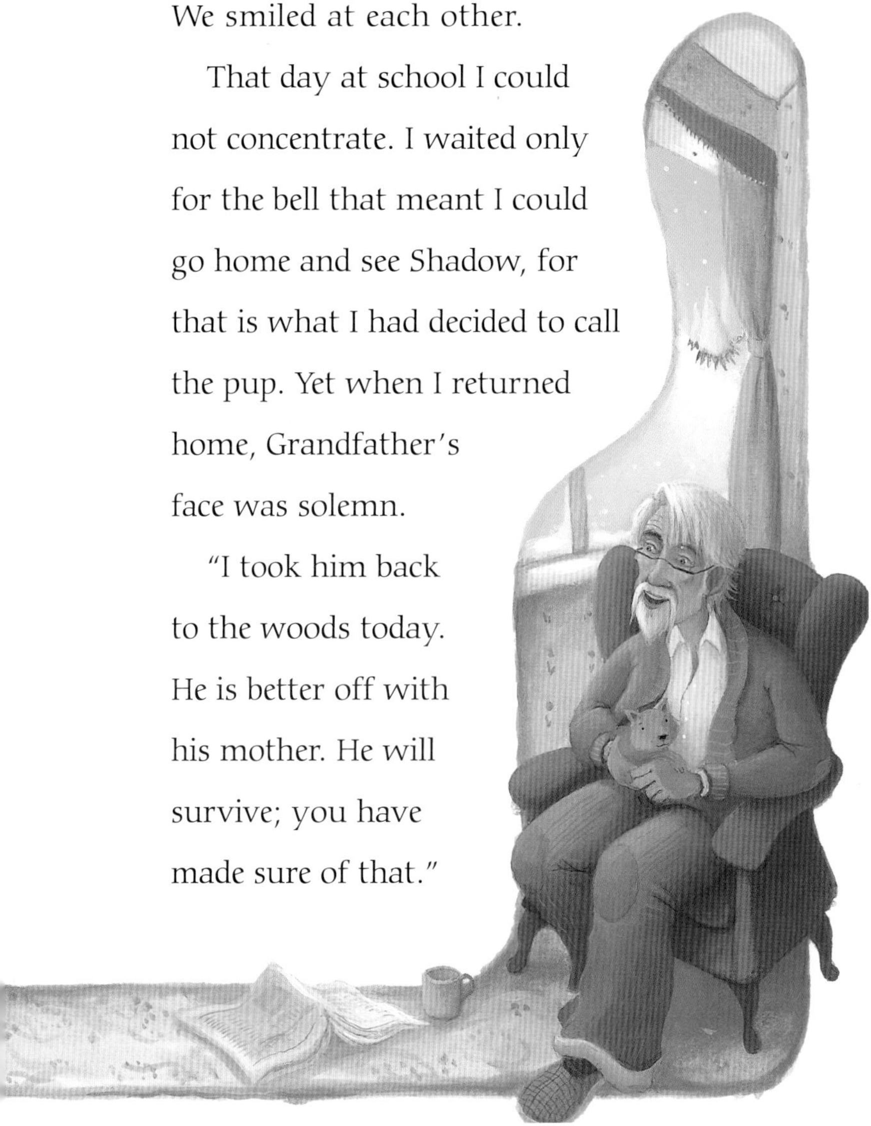

"Grandfather! How could you? What if she does not come for him?"

He tried to explain, but he was no match for a nine-year-old girl who would not listen to his patient words. I went to bed early that night, angry and silent. I could not believe what Grandfather had done. He did not care for me or for Shadow.

I knew in my heart that Grandfather had tried to do what was best, but I was not interested in his grown-up thoughts. A nine-year-old girl can also be right, and when

Shadow stepped in front of me on my way home from school the next day, I didn't need persuading that I was. At first he circled warily around me, but then he followed me, helped along by the crusts from my lunch, which I had not eaten to show Grandfather how much he had hurt me.

Grandfather seemed puzzled but not angry when he saw us approaching the cottage. He came outside, wiping his hands on his apron.

"See, Grandfather! He has followed me all the way home!"

Grandfather's gray eyebrows arched slowly and his face brightened.

"Well, I suppose if his mother does not want him, then somebody will have to look after him." He opened the door of our cottage and we stepped out of the snow, leaving the gathering darkness of the woods outside.

CHAPTER FIVE

SHADOW

AT FIRST, THE VILLAGERS SAID THAT Grandfather was crazy to let a girl keep a wolf pup. Didn't he know that the mother would come looking for her baby? Didn't he realize the danger the village would be in while the pup was under our roof? Didn't he know how large pups grow?

Later that week a meeting was called in the village to which the children were not allowed to go. Grandfather returned late when I was in bed, though still awake, and I heard him muttering to himself downstairs in the kitchen.

I knew they had been discussing Shadow, but the next morning Grandfather would not speak about the meeting.

"It is nothing, Maria. Those people think they can tell me what to do, but I have lived here longer than any of them."

That day school ended for the winter holidays. The winter before had been a time of freedom — each day brought games in the snow, laughter, and long treks through the woods of our snowbound valley with my friends. But that winter I stayed close by the cottage, spending most days with Grandfather and Shadow. At first Shadow followed me wherever I went, his tiny legs bounding in and out of the thick snow. Within a few weeks, he had grown so quickly on the milk and bread we gave him that Grandfather brought home

some meat and I fed him tiny scraps, which he gobbled up greedily.

"And us with barely enough to feed ourselves!" Grandfather grumbled. But I knew that he loved Shadow almost as much as I did.

Shadow was a willing pupil. By the time the heaviest of the snows had fallen and we had begun to watch for the first signs of spring, Shadow was running and playing. He soon learned to walk next to me and to come back when I called. Some nights we would lie together by the stove, listening to the wind in the chimney, and I would smooth his fur with the wooden brush that Grandfather had made for him.

We soon learned to keep Shadow away from the village. The few neighbors who saw us together that winter shook their heads ruefully. The children, however, were not as cold as the adults; they wanted to know all about Shadow. Some disobeyed the warnings of their parents and came secretly to see him — if Grandfather was out of the way. They seemed as afraid of him as they were of Shadow, regardless of how often I told them of his kindness.

One evening Grandfather made me stay at the table after supper.

"You know we have to make plans, Maria. You must go back to school soon and you will not be able to look after Shadow."

"Well, you will be here with him."

Grandfather nodded thoughtfully.

"Yes, but I have my work to do. What do you think we should do?"

I wasn't used to Grandfather asking my opinion, but when it came to Shadow, he seemed to think the decisions were mine. I thought carefully.

"Perhaps we should tie him up in the old goat pen? He would be safe there if we mended it properly and maybe you could look in on him from time to time?" I suggested.

Grandfather smiled and stroked my hair.

"Of course." He looked past me toward a dark corner of the room where the candlelight couldn't reach. "You are growing up so fast, my girl," he said, a faraway look in his eyes.

Chapter Six

Spring Arrives

SO IT HAPPENED THAT I HELPED Grandfather to mend the goat pen. On the first morning of school, after an early walk in the woods, I led Shadow to the pen and tied a rope gently around his neck. He looked at it curiously, sniffing the coils on the ground. But he soon discovered he could trot around the pen, and I crept quietly away as he explored his new surroundings.

In the playground before school, there was much excited conversation about Shadow, but never within the hearing of an adult. As we waited for the sound of the bell, a small crowd gathered around me, begging for details. What was he eating now? Did he howl at the moon? Where did he sleep? Was I ever frightened? I attempted answers to as many questions as I could, until the teacher came out, ringing the bell urgently, to see what the fuss was about. As the crowd slowly drifted away under her sharp gaze, she noticed me at its center and cast me a disapproving look.

One evening a few days later, there was a knock on the door. It was the village butcher. "Sebastian," he said, nodding at Grandfather.

"Good evening." Grandfather stood aside for him to come in.

The butcher shook his head. "No, no. I will not stay. I just thought...I had these scraps to throw away and..." His voiced trailed away as he caught sight of Shadow by the stove, watching the two adults closely with his sleek eyes.

"Thank you." Grandfather took the bag that the butcher held out. "It is most welcome. Will you stay to eat with us?"

"No, my family is expecting me. Thank you." He smiled at me and I smiled back. As he turned to leave, he hesitated and turned back.

"Sebastian? I don't want you to think that

you are not welcome in the village. People can be harsh, but they respect you still. For what it's worth, I think it's a fine animal."

Grandfather nodded solemnly and touched his cap.

"Good night, and thank you again."

As the green of spring and then summer began slowly to invade the valley, Shadow grew swiftly to the size of an adult wolf. He had begun sometimes to slip his rope, and Grandfather's attention, and I'd find him waiting outside school for me late in the day.

One warm afternoon, I looked out the classroom window and saw the butcher throwing meat scraps into a garbage can behind his shop. Sitting in class was hard for me that day and the warmth of the classroom was making it difficult to concentrate. I glanced back to the front of the room as the teacher wrote on the chalkboard, but I was already lost.

Outside I could see Shadow lying by the school gate, his head suddenly upright and alert as he caught the smell of the meat. The butcher stopped and looked around and, when he thought nobody was watching, he edged slowly toward Shadow and threw something to him. I couldn't stop my laughter as Shadow leaped up and the butcher fell backward in his hurry to get to his shop.

"Stand up and explain yourself, girl!"

The eyes of my classmates followed mine to the scene outside, and several children snickered.

The next day I saw the butcher repeat his favor and by the end of that week, Shadow had won his first adult friend in the village. That was the start of the thaw. Over time, as Shadow began to follow me everywhere, the villagers got to know him. At first, the older women shuddered as they passed by, but as I began to spend more of each day in the village with Shadow alongside me, their wariness turned gradually to curiosity. Carefully, meanwhile, my friends began to bend the rule about not playing with Shadow until eventually their parents had all but forgotten it.

Chapter Seven

The Traders

SHADOW BECAME MY CLOSEST friend. I told him everything, shared all my thoughts and fears, my hopes and dreams, my regrets and triumphs. And I always told him that the best thing I ever did in my life was pick him up in my arms on that cold afternoon in the woods. Those summer days were some of the happiest times I can remember, lying on the hillside in the warm sun with my friends, Shadow asleep at our feet, making plans for the days ahead.

One day, traders from over the mountains

arrived in our village.

They set up tents and stalls to sell their furs and tools, and each evening as the sun set they lit a large fire and sat around it, telling stories and making jokes. In the evenings, their camp was a magnet to the villagers, particularly to us children. There was something magical about the dancing flames and the laughter that drew us in each night, and the traders were happy to let us join them until our parents called us home.

The first time the traders saw Shadow they were surprised. "Is he a good wolf?" they asked, as they nervously patted his neck. Shadow enjoyed the company; I could tell by

the way
that he raised
his front paws slightly
off the ground from time
to time. Over the next few
days, the traders became fond
of Shadow and often fed him
scraps of food so that he
would come to see them again.

One of the traders, though,
was a large, miserable man
who seemed to keep himself
apart from the others.
He observed Shadow
carefully and

I didn't like the way he stared with his piercing blue eyes, never smiling, never patting or feeding Shadow as the other traders did.

On their last night in the village, the traders gathered around the fire outside their tents, and all the children and the villagers came to share the evening with them. The trader with the piercing eyes passed me in the glow of the fire and stopped.

"That wolf will turn on you one day, girl." He put his face closer to mine and I felt frightened. Even in the dim glow of the firelight, I could see his fat, stubbly chin and smell the alcohol on his breath. "Let me take him. I can sell his fur easily. I'll give you good money for him." He looked down at Shadow, who was standing at my heels, and laughed.

Chapter Eight

An Offer

JUST THEN, AS THE TRADER STOOD face to face with me, I heard a familiar cough and turned to see Grandfather standing in the dark beyond the glow of the fire, watching us carefully.

"Ah, here is your grandfather!" the trader said, and walked over to him. I saw them talk but could not hear what they said. I think, though, that the trader must have offered Grandfather a large amount of money for Shadow, because Grandfather scratched his head for a while and looked serious. The trader became animated and Grandfather glanced over at me. I smiled at him and put my hand out to feel Shadow's wet nose. Grandfather spoke again. Then they both shrugged their shoulders and smiled. The man walked slowly past me, touched Shadow lightly on the ear and winked at me, before moving away to speak to someone else.

"Grandfather, what did he say?" I asked.

"Oh nothing, Maria," Grandfather answered dismissively. "He was not serious."

But I knew differently, and the memory of the man's breath on my face and his plans for Shadow made me shudder. I told Grandfather what he had asked me.

"Yes," Grandfather admitted, "he asked me the same thing."

"You said no, of course?" I asked.

Grandfather hesitated, and

looked over to where the man was now standing, holding a bottle in his hand and talking to one of our neighbors.

"The money he offered would certainly have helped us. But no, Maria. I am not as hard-hearted as you might think." He tickled my chin gently and I giggled.

The next morning when I went to the village with Shadow, the traders were gone.

Chapter Nine

The Storyteller

LIFE CARRIED ON. THE SEASONS passed, and by the following summer, Shadow had grown into an adult. He still slept by the stove in our kitchen, and he still waited for me every day after school. The traders returned for another week, and they laughed to see Shadow still by my side.

"He's nearly as big as you, girl!"

"What have you been feeding him?"

They patted his head and squeezed his ears, which Shadow suffered patiently.

The large trader who had offered us money

for Shadow arrived alone to the campfire two evenings after the others.

"Hey, Pascal! What kept you?" one of the traders asked. Someone in the darkness said something I could not hear, and the traders all laughed. Pascal scowled and threw his bags on the ground.

"Here, Pascal. This will lighten you up. Give us a smile!" A man stepped forward and held out a bottle. Pascal grunted and took the bottle to a loud cheer from the traders.

Later, I listened to a story told by one of the women. She told of a boy who was lost in the mountains and was cared for by a pack of wolves. There were gasps of horror when the storyteller described how the wolves first discovered the boy, lying by a rock, asleep in the snow. Everyone assumed the wolves

would rip him to shreds. The storyteller often used Shadow to describe the wolves, and I was sure that she was making up the story just for him and me. At the end, the boy was returned safely to his parents. Everyone loved the story and the storyteller received a large round of applause.

"Come on, Maria. It's time to go home." Grandfather placed his hand on my head and stroked my hair. "You look tired." We said goodnight to the company and walked off into the darkness.

Suddenly, on the rough path out of the village, in the darkness of the trees to our right, we heard a rustling.

Grandfather stopped and listened. There was nothing.

"Maybe just a rabbit or something," he said. Still, he gripped my hand a little more tightly as we continued. As we approached our cottage, where Grandfather had left a lantern shining on the porch, there was another noise, and this time a voice spoke from behind us.

Chapter Ten

A Meeting in the Woods

"I'M SORRY. I DIDN'T MEAN TO STARTLE you," the voice said.

We turned quickly. Although we were used to being alone in the darkness of the woods, it was unusual for anybody else to be out here so late at night.

A figure emerged from the darkness to reveal the owner of the soft, melodic voice. I recognized her instantly. It was the storyteller. She smiled and knelt by Shadow, who whined and licked her face vigorously. She laughed.

"You! I've missed you!" She tickled his belly and he rolled over.

The storyteller stood up and looked directly at me with her sleek gray eyes. She seemed so beautiful to me, there in the moonlight. There was something so still and calm about her face. Something that reminded me a little of Shadow, when I'd look up sometimes and catch him quietly watching me from his place by the stove.

"Good evening, again, miss," Grandfather said, recognizing her. "We are not used to company here at this hour. Are you walking alone in the woods?" Grandfather seemed concerned.

"I am used to it. Humans are too afraid of darkness, in my opinion. It is my favorite time, when night falls." She turned back to me. "You enjoyed my story this evening?" I nodded heartily.

"Good," she said. "Good...I told it for you." She touched my hair gently. "You have been so kind to him, and he is so big now! He was lucky that *you* found him, instead of Pascal!" Shadow rubbed his head against her hand and she held his ear between her fingers as though they had been friends for a long time.

"Perhaps you would like to come inside for a while?" Grandfather motioned toward the cottage with his arm.

"Thank you, but I must return to my family. We have been separated for too long already." She smiled and bowed her head. "Good evening, sir. Maria, you are also lucky to have such a kind grandfather to look after you!" I reached out and took Grandfather's hand in mine. The storyteller turned and was quickly lost to sight.

We went inside and Grandfather busied himself warming milk for me.

"Grandfather? How did she know my name?" I looked out of the window into the impenetrable blackness.

He stopped stirring the milk for a moment and looked thoughtful.

"I don't know. She must be the wife of one of the traders, I suppose. Shadow certainly liked her." Grandfather bent down and gave Shadow a pat. "Didn't you?"

Shadow lay by the stove with his head on his paws, watching the door. The milk boiled over and the hiss made Grandfather jump up quickly. I laughed and let Shadow out the door, and Grandfather grinned back at me as he mopped the milk off the stove. It was then that, for the first time, we heard Shadow howl — the saddest and yet the most beautiful sound I had ever heard.

Chapter Eleven

Where is He?

ONE MORNING THE FOLLOWING spring, I woke from a strange dream about Shadow that I could not quite remember. I rose and went to the kitchen. The last snow was falling through sunshine and the world outside was alive with shadows. As I turned from the window, I noticed Shadow's empty place by the stove and asked Grandfather where he was.

"He was not here when I came in from the woodshed. He must have gone to the woods. Don't worry; he'll come back. He always does."

And Grandfather was right. Shadow was quite independent now and often went into the woods alone. He was gone for long periods, sometimes days at a time, but he always came back, briars and seed cases stuck to his fur. He would allow me to pull them off gently, one by one, as I sat on the porch and he lay at my feet.

But three days passed and Shadow had still not returned to the cottage. I could tell that Grandfather was worried.

"Let's wait until morning. He may return; it is cold outside tonight."

I waited all night for the sound of Shadow scratching at the door but in the gray half-light of dawn, I slept restlessly.

He was gone.

Chapter Twelve

Over the Mountains

GRANDFATHER MADE ME GO TO school, but before I left he promised to look for Shadow.

"Why would he leave us?" I fretted.

"Well, my child. Nobody owns Shadow. He is a wild animal and if he wants to go who are we to stop him?"

I was sure that Pascal had come and taken him for his fur, and I told Grandfather this.

Soon after this, as I was getting ready for school on a cruel spring morning, Grandfather came to a decision.

"I'll walk over the mountain to the traders' village and ask if anyone's seen Shadow," he said to me.

"Let me come, too!" I pleaded, but Grandfather shook his head. I stood on the porch and watched as Grandfather toiled through the snow with his best boots and walking stick.

I waited for a while, narrowing my eyes against the white snow. Then I followed at a safe distance. But after a few miles, he turned around too quickly and caught me hiding behind a tree.

"You must love that wolf, Maria," he grumbled as the snow whipped his ears and he pulled his scarf up around them. Large flakes of snow were sticking to his gray beard.

I reached up and shook them off. "I do."

We smiled at each other and he lifted me up onto his back.

The walk to the village was long and hard, but Grandfather never complained. We ate bread in the shelter of a large boulder as the snow scurried past. Later, as we neared the village, heading down from the mountain pass through the trees, we saw a woman coming in the other direction, wrapped against the snow in a thick, gray fur coat. She recognized us first.

"Maria!" she called out to me. I peered through the snowflakes. "I remember you, and your wolf. Shadow, isn't that what you called him? Do you remember me? I am the one who told the wolf story."

I tried to smile, but it was already taking all my willpower to hold back the tears in my throat. She seemed to realize something was wrong and looked at Grandfather.

"She is upset," Grandfather explained. "Shadow is missing. We came to look for him here, and to ask if your friends have seen him."

The woman lightly touched my hair, just as she had on that night in the woods the previous summer. Her damp fur coat smelled of the forest.

"He is not here." She said it so clearly, with such assurance that I looked up quickly and caught her eye. She watched me with the stillness of wolves.

"How do you know?" I asked, the tears starting to rise.

"I know wolves. He is somewhere safe, with others of his own kind. You must not worry.

You did everything you could for him and he is safe, thanks to you."

"You don't know that!" I cried, and the tears flooded out. I buried my head in Grandfather's coat.

"You must trust me, Maria."

I heard her words, but they meant nothing. My whole world felt black.

Chapter Thirteen

Night Walk

WHEN WE ARRIVED IN THE village, we were disappointed. At the local inn, some of the traders remembered Shadow but they had not seen him since the day they left.

The best-trained dog they ever knew, they said, and laughed.

"What a star he was. A better dog than my old mongrel!"

When I tugged at Grandfather's coat, he reluctantly questioned them about Pascal.

Again they laughed.

"Pascal would not be able to trap that clever wolf, not with all the spirits he drinks in a day! He doesn't even own a gun!"

Grandfather seemed to accept their word quickly and somehow I believed them, too. They gave us food and we rested glumly for a while by the warmth of the fire.

We walked home in bright moonlight. The snow had stopped falling and the sky was clear. Grandfather held my hand tightly as we followed the path carefully through the woods, across the shadows of trees, between the noises of the night. His hand was warm and I wasn't afraid with him there.

"You know, Maria, it is strange."

Even in the strange glow of moonlight, I could see that he was puzzled by something.

"What is it?"

"When you were asleep by the fire I was talking to the traders. I told them about the woman we met on the way here, the one we saw at our cottage last summer, the gray-eyed storyteller."

"What about her?" I asked.

"Well, I described her as well as I could, but nobody knew her. They remembered her story, but swore it was one of our villagers who had told it."

As we drew closer to home, we talked about Shadow, his funny habits, and how much we missed him. I cried again, and Grandfather lifted me gently to his face. I saw his tears too.

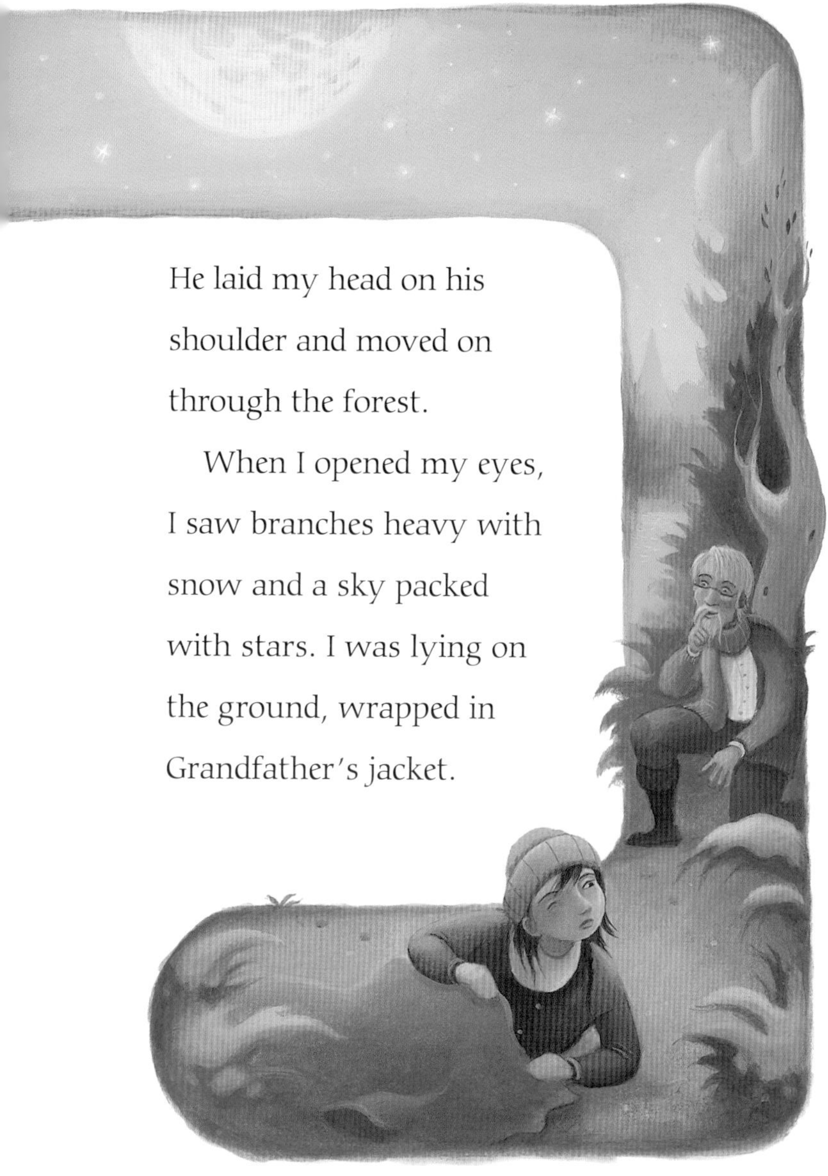

He laid my head on his shoulder and moved on through the forest.

When I opened my eyes, I saw branches heavy with snow and a sky packed with stars. I was lying on the ground, wrapped in Grandfather's jacket.

Then I saw Grandfather standing by a tree in the moonlight. When I called his name, he turned quickly, put his finger to his lips and beckoned me to come. He was watching something from behind his tree.

"Look." He held me close with one arm and, with the other, pointed at something in the distance. "There."

CHAPTER FOURTEEN

THE WOLVES AT THE RIVER

AT FIRST, MY EYES FOUND IT HARD to make anything out in the moonlight, except for the shadows thrown by the trees. Then I saw the river and heard the rushing sound of its meltwaters racing down the hillside to the big river in our valley that would take them on to the sea, many miles away.

"It's a river, Grandfather."

He smiled gently as he took my head between his hands and turned it to one side, directing my line of sight.

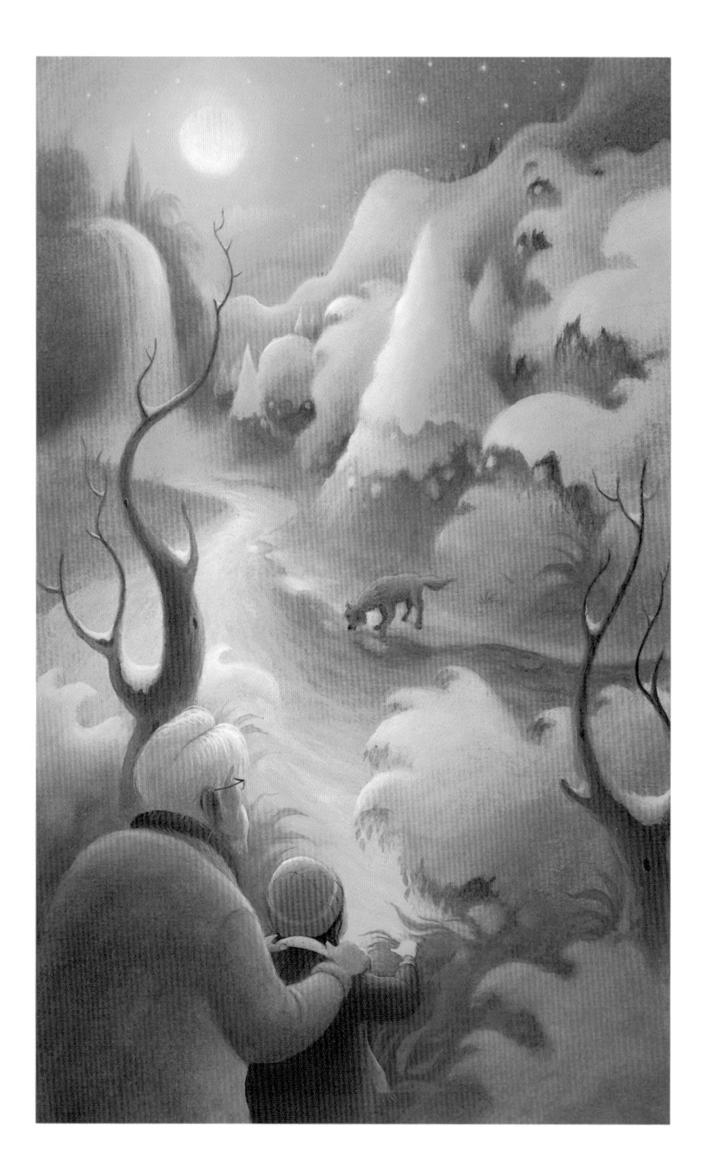

"There. Now do you see?"

On the far side of the river, I could see a large shape moving slowly in the moonlight. And as my eyes became used to the new view, I realized it was a wolf. My heart jolted in my chest.

"Is it him?" I whispered.

A large clump of snow slid from a branch and fell to the ground, making us jump, then laugh. Grandfather shook his head.

"No, it's too small. I think it's an adult female, a mother."

We watched in the hush of the night forest as the wolf lapped at the racing water, sometimes walking right into the river and standing against the flow. I gasped as a fish leaped out of the water, its silver back flashing in the moonlight.

"She's drinking," I said.

Grandfather nodded.

"Come on. It's late. You'll catch cold."

He lifted me up. I kept my eyes on the wolf. Suddenly, she stopped drinking and swung around, sniffing the air, and looked in our direction. As Grandfather turned to leave, I noticed several more wolves moving to the river's edge. And then...Grandfather stifled a cry as I tugged his beard sharply.

"Look! Look! It *is* him. It's Shadow. There! We've found him!"

Grandfather took my hand from his beard and squeezed it firmly.

"Be quiet, child!" he whispered urgently. "You will frighten them, and I, for one, do not wish to be chased home by a family of wolves!" Then he nodded, smiling.

"Yes, Maria. We've found him. And look! I think he has become a father."

We watched as Shadow and the rest of the pack, including three pups, joined the mother in the river and drank from the rushing water. I followed his every movement, aching to call out his name, certain that he would come running into my outstretched arms.

But I remained silent, and I could feel Grandfather's heartbeat through his shirt. The pack left the river and stood on the bank, shaking themselves and licking their fur — all except Shadow who stayed in the water, looking intently in our direction.

Grandfather turned quietly to go. I strained against him, wanting to stay a little longer.

"Come, Maria. We must leave him." He walked slowly, carefully away, toward the path that would lead us home.

Somehow, the separation hurt a little less now that I'd seen Shadow happy with his family. When I turned briefly for a last glimpse, he was still there, standing in the river with the cold water racing around his legs. I knew he was watching us with his beautiful gray eyes, and I waved. When Grandfather heard Shadow howl at the moon he began to trot, and I laughed quietly to myself.

Back at the cottage, Grandfather wrapped me in a blanket and sat me on his lap by the stove, where Shadow used to lie at night. As the melting snow fell heavily from the branches of the trees onto the wooden roof above us, Grandfather stroked my hair softly, telling me stories of my parents, of when I was a baby, until my eyes began to flicker and I fell asleep in the warmth of his arms.

CHAPTER FIFTEEN

BACK HOME

IN THE MONTHS THAT FOLLOWED, I walked many times alone in the woods and mountains, hoping for another glimpse of Shadow. That summer, I sat every night on the porch, listening to the wolves in the mountains, straining my ears to recognize his call among the distant howling. Sometimes Grandfather came out and carved wood by my side. He knew what I was thinking, and I knew that he was listening too, but he never spoke of Shadow. He would just sit for a while, watching my sadness drift slowly away into the night air, until a time came when he'd touch my hair lightly.

"Time for bed, Maria."

I often thought back to the day when I'd picked Shadow up in my arms from the deep snow and carried him home to the warm kitchen. It seemed so long ago. I would soon be twelve, and the world felt like a different place to me. I knew now that I would never see Shadow again, no matter how far from our valley I wandered. But I could still feel him there among the trees and mountain tracks, in the rushing of the wind, the swirling of the winter snowstorms and the racing of the rivers in springtime.